D1088986

# THE MAGIC CARPET

## and the

# CEMENT WALL

Richard M. Vixen

## FOR KIDS  FROM 8 TO 92

## illustrated by
# gregg davidson

**AVANT-GARDE CREATIONS**
Box 30161  Eugene, OR 97403

Library of Congress Catalog Card Number:
77-93804

First Printing:  August 1978
ISBN: 0-930182-06-5 Hardcover;
       0-930182-05-7 Paperback

Printed  in  the  United  States  of  America

Dear Reader,

Hello. My name is Linda. If you've read the kinds of books most kids have, you'll probably end up feeling that my role in this story is the "fairy godmother" of Lindsay and Sammy.

It's true I love them and help them and I appear to them from out of nowhere. But I am most assuredly NOT their fairy godmother. I am simply myself. And I came from---

Well, you'll see soon enough. Now, about the 2 sweet kids, Lindsay and Sammy.

Lindsay is 8 and is in 3rd grade at the Phil M. Fullabean's Elementary School. She is very lively and brave and fun. And sometimes "hard to manage". At least that's what her school and parents think. I don't. I think she's perfect exactly as she is. Her spirit is one of the most lovely things about the young lady. Her blond hair and brown eyes and impish grin all contribute to her loveliness. Lindsay is quite Alive!

Some parents and teachers like only quiet, orderly, obedient, robot-like kids. They might find Lindsay not "appealing" but "trying". Or downright frustrating. You see, she isn't about to be tied down or "managed". Isn't it funny how she can be seen as lovable by some people and aggravating or "bad" by others?

Sammy is 8 and he's also nearly 9, which is a good kind of 8 to be if you often wish you'd hurry up and get to be 16 or 18 so that you could run your own life. He's in the 3rd grade also. He has brown hair and brown eyes. Sammy is very bright. This means he can be very sly. He can make people think he's feeling one way when he's actually feeling another. He doesn't WISH to be dishonest, mind you. But sometimes he gets punished for letting people see how he really feels.

After all, a person can't help how he FEELS! No amount of punishment will make him quit feeling that way. What the spankings do is to make him feel angry and hurt and guilty and afraid IN ADDITION TO feeling the very same way he started out feeling!

So Sammy uses his brains to make his surroundings more pleasant. He isn't a "liar". He feels he is a good kid. He knows darn well that he doesn't DESERVE most of the ill-treatment that comes his way, so he finds clever ways to avoid most of it.

Even animals want to survive and be happy, and when things get rough they find ways to avoid dangerous or even just unpleasant surroundings.

Sammy and Lindsay are brother and sister and live under constant fear of their dad having another one of his "bad days". When he does, he takes it out on his wife and kids both. So clever Sammy is often trying to keep himself and Lindsay out of trouble. And that's the way it happens.

They need each other. Lindsay needs Sammy to help keep her from getting punished so often. He knows when to calm her down around parents and teachers. Sammy thinks too much sometimes. He needs Lindsay to help "pull him out of his brain", where it is easy for him to hide. He is secure there. But if Sammy lives out of his brain too much of the time he can really get confused:

He might start BELIEVING that the "good little robot" act he puts on is really him. And that would make him stop feeling happy and alive.

They sure feel lucky that they ended up as brother and sister. They are very affectionate and trusting with each other, are the best of pals, and have oodles of fun together.

Whenever things get rough at home, Sammy and Lindsay retreat to one of their "forts". These are little spaces the kids have created where they can go to do their own thing, without anyone bothering them. They have big imaginations, and at their forts they can make all their fantasies be true.

Fort No. 1 is their treehouse, which Lindsay has fallen out of twice. Well, not really twice. The second time she had on a cape and was being "Supergirl". But broken arms are often part of growing up.

Fort No. 2 is their camp, which is a little cleared-out spot hidden by some trees and bushes in the park nearby. It has a ring of rocks and a little pit where they roast marshmallows at times. It is a block away and they often have to sneak off to it because their father thinks they'll "get into less trouble" if they stay on the block. It is very peaceful at their camp.

Fort No. 3 is the attic hideaway. They'd walled off a little section of the attic with junk, so that they would have to crawl through a maze of boxes and trunks and furniture just to end up in their private little spot. It feels very secure and cozy there. It is a great place to hide when dad "has a bad day". Call and threaten as he might, they never give away their hideaway.

Fort No. 4 is the closet of their room.

They live in a small inexpensive house in a small inexpensive neighborhood. It has only 2 bedrooms. Mom and dad use the downstairs one, and the kids use the upstairs one. Dad is planning to build another bedroom within the next year. . . something about it "Not being healthy for little boys and girls to share the same room".

Now this unexplained decision is very upsetting to both Sammy and Lindsay. They are terribly fond of one another and this threat of separating them because it is "bad for them to be together" feels like the ultimate proof of what they'd always felt:

1) Dad is off his rocker.
2) It is unfair that children have to be helpless victims of dumb decisions made by adults.

He never asks THEM what THEIR feelings on the matter are! And if there is ONE thing in THEIR world that they are totally certain of, it is that it is perfectly right for them to be close to each other!

These sudden decisions seem so unfair that they have begun discussing plans to run away together in their secret forts. Just yesterday they'd gone to Mars to discuss it.

You see, the closet is whatever they WANT it to be. And it was a spaceship yesterday.

Anyway, dad is O.K. a lot of the time. But then he goes and---YOU know. Every family has not-so-nice things about it, as I'm sure you've noticed. I know this too, because I can---well, you'll see later. Kids almost ALWAYS end up drying tears and asking themselves: "Why does it have to be this way?" A few kids run away. Most kids daydream about it at times.

When dad is good part of the time and hateful part of the time, it's very confusing to Sammy and Lindsay. They wonder if they are "bad" or if they're just unlucky. It's a good thing Sammy is around to help Lindsay figure this one out, or she'd be very likely to start believing that she is a "bad" person, with all the punishments she gets or nearly gets.

Mom is such a nice lady. She never picks on the kids like dad sometimes does. But she also never stops him if he begins picking on her or the kids. She is a fine lady in the affection department, but lacks plenty in the strength department. Lindsay and Sammy are sure fond of her. But when she starts making "excuses" for "daddy's behavior", or when she talks about "his rough day at the office", they often politely excuse themselves and go to one of their forts.

So you can SEE how lucky they are to have each other.

At school they both do well. Lindsay is no dodo---she is quite smart. Her spirit is stronger than her brain, but that speaks for the largeness of her spirit, not the smallness of her brain. The teachers have her in and out of the principal's office because she is TOO lively for their tastes. But she has great fun playing with the other kids at school.

Sammy manages to stay out of trouble except for the times when he is a "smarty-pants" to the teachers, or when he plays one of his little tricks. He does things like hide the assignment book. The assignments are simple enough, but he just doesn't like someone telling him what he "should" do without ever asking HIM about it.

Now, Lindsay and Sammy are reaching an important point in their lives. More and more pressure is coming down upon them to be and act ways that don't feel right to them. They feel like they are backed up against a wall.

Their support of one another's feelings is the only thing that has "saved them" so far. It helps that mom is nice to them and at times even reads stories to them. But mom's affection doesn't protect the 2 lovable kids against dad's "bad days". Nor does she ever support them when they are up against unnecessary pressures from school.

So Sammy and Lindsay are on their own. A brave team with its back to the wall, making a last stand. . .trying not to give in to all these forces, fighting against pressures to become "good little robots", and trying to live by their feelings rather than letting themselves feel ONLY "what they SHOULD feel."

So now you have a view of the lives, feelings, and truths of Lindsay, Sammy, their family, their school, and the ever-increasing challenge that life has brought them.

Will this wonderful Dynamic Duo end up different from the way most people seem to end up, or----------------?

Love,
Linda

**O**nce upon a time there was a little boy and a little girl. The boy's name was Sammy. The girl's name was Lindsay. They were lovable children, and very close. Like right now, for example:

"Let's let it go!" shouted Sammy who was at the main dam. It was already full.

"No, not yet!" returned Lindsay, who was still building up the 2 minor dams up-"river". They loved playing "dam". The old leaves in the gutter made perfect dams for the rainwater if you built them up right. It had been raining off and on for 2 days and this morning it was really pouring. The air smelled fresh and clean.

All the gutters of the town of Plainville were full of water, and the water just couldn't wait to rush along until it poured into the nearest storm-drain. Lindsay and Sammy loved the whooshing sound that it made when it poured into the hungry mouths of the stormdrains.

To most of the townsfolk these Spring rains meant good crops, wet clothes, cleaner cars muddy shoes, and more T.V. But to some of the kids, especially Lindsay and Sammy, it meant *fun!*

They were sure glad it was Sunday, because otherwise they would have been sitting in school, fidgeting and hoping it would still be raining when they got out.

"How 'bout now?" called Sammy, who was eager for "The dam is bursting!"

Which is exactly what Lindsay suddenly screamed.

They both ran back upstream to the first and second little dams. Sammy "blew up" the first one, causing a small deluge of water to come pouring down the gutter, crashing into dam No. 2, which Lindsay "helped" the onrushing water burst.

The combined water from both dams was now rushing for the main dam, threatening to burst it as well!

"Neato!" screamed Lindsay, as the tidal wave of water rushed mercilessly into the big dam. Both kids had run full speed to the big dam and were all ready to help the wave do its best, AND worst! They both pounced, at just the right moment, on the main dam and now a torrent of flood-water descended upon the "unsuspecting town down the valley from the main dam".

The "mens and ladies" were hit without warning by the flood, but giants Sammy and Lindsay managed to save most of them from drowning. They still called these little dime-store people what they did when they were 3 years old. And they still played with them. Because it was *fun.*

All of a sudden from out of a bush flew a 3-inch rubber man wearing a cape. It was Superman to the rescue! Supergirl flew out of another bush, and the 2 flying 3" Superheroes rushed for the second town about to be deluged by the dam-waters. There were only 4 people in that leaf-hill town, and at the very moment the flood came down upon them, each superhero grabbed 2 people and flew them safely to high ground. The town was saved!

Lindsay and Sammy cheered and sighed and giggled happily. They loved being the cause of things, and loved setting things up the way *they* wanted them, with no teachers or parents telling them about what they "should do".

Eventually "dam-bursting" wore out, so they retreated to the house, put their slickers and rain hats and boots neatly in the hall, and had crunchy-creamy-yummy peanut-butter-and-cracker sandwiches, washed down with milk.

Since no one was around, they did their "music ritual". They blasted a "neat" radio station and danced around the living room in trances like they were floating at zero gravity like those Spacelab guys had done on T.V.

This particular ritual was one of those secret and special parts of their lives. They couldn't do it very often, because dad would forbid it. And even if only mom had been home, this was a *secret* ritual, and they had no intention of showing it to her or anyone.

The loud wild rhythms and pretty chords combined to make them feel like they were weightless, or "drunk" or *something*. They whirled, floated, danced and rolled around until they were exhausted.

"Isn't it neato to have all this room to dance in, Sammy?" puffed Lindsay.

"I'll say.  No *interference!*" replied Sammy.  It was quite a word for an 8-year-old, except for one thing:  Sammy was very bright, and was reading at the 8th grade level.  But whenever his teachers started talking about moving him up a grade or two, since he was so smart, a very strange thing happened:  Sammy became dumb!  But this was no accident.

Sammy knew that his super-spirited sister Lindsay would be in no end of trouble if he wasn't in her class with her.  He was her----"brake pedal".  And he loved her and *preferred* being in the same grade as she was.  In addition, he knew that he'd always get called "that little smarty" if he was in 5th grade.  He got picked on enough at home; so he wasn't going to be teased at school too, if he could help it.

Besides he always read whatever books he wanted.  He didn't need to be in a higher grade to read what he found interesting.

Sammy remembered sitting in the principal's office, looking at the faces of his teacher and principal as they urged him to get moved up a grade.  These 2 "adults" were *so* sure that *they* knew what was best for him.  They tried to make him feel like a silly, foolish kid who couldn't possibly know what *he* preferred.

It had made Sammy angry.  But he didn't let it show---he was too smart.  He knew getting mad could get him in even more trouble.

Why couldn't adults understand?  Why were they so blind and dumb?  Couldn't they see how terribly unhappy he would be if he suddenly had to put up with 2 or 3 times as much pressure or 2 or 3 times as much getting picked on, or both?  They were *so* darn sure of themselves---*so* positive that *they* were *right!*  Why didn't they care about how he felt?

Sammy was lying on the floor, staring at the ceiling, remembering things:  *Sure* he knew it would help him "learn" faster if they moved him up!  *Sure* he knew he'd be able to feel "proud" of himself for being so "gifted" (what a word!).  And he could get to high school a year or 2 before everyone else in his class!  But SO WHAT?

This was just school-talk; it was all just *words.*  What about his *feelings?*  Yes, there it was again.  This was where all these "adults" were just plain dumb.  How could they know so much about some things---but also be so dumb about others?!

Lindsay didn't like to see Sammy sad.  So after giving him time to get done with his thinking, she sat on his stomach and held down his arms and said playfully:

"Come on---I see your face."  No response.  Her hand played mousie and walked around on his chest.

"Here comes the mousie---here comes the mousie---come on, Samwich, I see your face!"  The mousie found an armpit and his face found a smile and she tickled and giggled and suddenly he came to life . . . and the wrestling match was on.

It was Friday. They were walking home from school. It was 5 blocks. They were worried. They hadn't really been bad, and they knew it, but the teacher thought so. *They'd* felt *good* about finally saying how they felt about something important. It felt good to let it out. And yet, with the truth would come the consequences.

The other kids in their class thought they "were just asking for it", as Tommy had put it---after school.

And the teacher *knew* they were asking for it. So she gave it to them. First a scolding, which they let go in one ear and out the other, as usual.

But the note: *that* had to go home to their parents. Mom would understand. But dad---. They were wondering out loud to each other if the teacher would send home notes if she knew the way dad *was*. They supposed not.

Anyway, to make a long story short, they both got a beating that night after dad came home. He was having one of his "bad days" and they tried hard to stay away from him, but it didn't work!

Later, while they were on Sammy's bed comforting each other and drying their tears, mom came up and told them that she was sorry it happened and "they just needed to turn the other cheek and realize that everyone has his bad days".

"That was an awful spanking to get just because of that dumb note," Sammy sobbed into his mother's comforting arm.

"Uh---no, dear, he---he hasn't seen it yet---," mom corrected.

They might have know it! It was just another unreasonable misery at the hands of mean old dad! He usually used something for an "excuse". This time he hadn't bothered to invent one.

"Are you gonna-----?" began Lindsay, looking up worriedly at her mother.

"You know I have to show it to him, hon. I can't be *dishonest* with him," mom answered.

"Oooohhh! *You don't understand!*" Lindsay hollered at her mother, and then turned over on the bed---with her back to her.

"Lin, I love you---you know that---but I just can't---I can't----I shouldn't---"

"Go away, mom," Lindsay sighed deadly.

After a bit more discussion, consisting mostly of excuse-making and more "go-away"'s, mom left. Just before she got to the door she reminded them:

"You know, a person can't change the way things are. Whatever is, is. You just have to make the best of it."

Sammy felt a nasty tension---he was watching his angry sister eyeball the alarm clock and knew that she was on the verge of firing it at the door mom had just closed. He knew he'd have to-------

Her arm lunged. Sammy pounced on her before she had a chance to throw it.

"No, no---*don't*, Lindsay!" Sammy frantically whispered. He felt her relax her grip, and he turned her around and cuddled her and she began to sob. It wasn't like her to cry so much. Part of him felt like he was cuddling himself as well as his lovable but unhappy sister.

Hoping that he'd be too guilty to hit them anymore so soon after the spankings, their mother handed the note to her husband immediately. It read:

"Dear Mr. and Mrs. Jones,
        Your children were a bit unmanageable in school today. I believe I have everything under control now, however.

                        Yours very truly,

                        Evelyn Liverwurst"

Dad was too interested in a "Gunsmoke" rerun to give the note too much notice. He merely shouted at the top of his lungs for a half minute, without even turning his head in the direction of the stairway that led up to their room. He let them know that they weren't going out of their room for the whole weekend, except to eat or use the toilet.

So here they were, grounded, with a beautiful warm Spring weekend in May coming up tomorrow. Why was life so hateful?

Lindsay was remembering the incident at school. Mrs. Liverwurst had asked Sammy to give a state capital. He'd given it to her but then had started to politely suggest that it might be real interesting for everyone if all the kids got a chance to say what they *wanted* to learn, in addition to having to learn stuff like state capitals, since they seemed like such a waste of time. But before Sammy or anyone else got a chance to say what it was he or she wanted to learn, Sammy was hauled up to the desk and scolded for calling his studies a "waste of time".

She simply couldn't contain herself. Lindsay had stood up, and without raising her hand had said:

"Mrs. Liverwurst, I'd like to learn about people, about what causes hate, and---"

"Sit down this instant, young lady!" scolded the already-scolding teacher.

"But I *would!!*" shouted Lindsay, who unfortunately punctuated this sentence with a flying geography book, which hit the blackboard and tumbled to the floor.

What a scolding she received for *that!* And what a strong right arm our Lindsay has!

That night they slept in Lindsay's bed together, holding each other and feeling like the world was against them. Just before either child was asleep, a very strange thing happened. A very spooky thing.

Sammy and Lindsay were facing the paneled wall on the east side of the room. Lindsay's arms were around Sammy, who was in front of her. She was nearly asleep, but a tiny sliding noise (or was it her imagination?) forced open her eyes. She looked at the wall and imagined (?) she saw a panel open and a wispy, hazy, ghostlike face appear for a second. A smiling, sweet, lovely female face. She started to move her right arm in order to awaken Sammy, but the "spirit" was gone in a flash. There was nothing to show him. She thought she heard faint, distant, bubbling laughter.

The strangest part of this was that Sammy was facing the same direction, almost asleep; and he also heard the noise, opened his eyes, and saw or imagined he saw *the very same thing!*

The next morning Lindsay woke Sammy up and asked him with restrained excitement if anything unusual had happened to him last night. He wiped the cobwebs out of his eyes and looked at her and thought for a moment. Then he told her about the ghost-lady. Lindsay's hands fondled and explored the soft, sleek border on the pink blanket they were beneath, as she listened to his response with amazement.

"Me *too!* It happened to me *too!*" exclaimed Lindsay. She was very excited. Sammy was confused. He wanted to make sense out of it. He wanted to understand.

"If we *both* saw it, it simply *couldn't* be imagination, Lindsay," he stated.

"You mean----it really happened?!" asked Lindsay, eyes widened in astonishment.

"It's the only explanation. Oh gosh, that---that means we saw a ghost! That means there are ghosts!" Sammy was excited too.

"Oh neato, Samwich! Ghosts! Real ghosts!" And with this she hugged Sammy and rolled around on the bed with him chuckling delightedly.

"Wait a second---", and Sammy was suddenly staring at the ceiling as if recalling something. "What did you dream last night, Q.T.?" (This was short for "cutie" and Sammy used it affectionately at times.)

Lindsay thought hard but couldn't remember.

"Well, I dreamed I was in a really neat family and everyone just loved everyone ever so much, and there were lots of moms and dads to be with and I was so happy, and-----and the dream ended by sort of melting---or bursting into----into----a bunch----no, a shower of golden rain!" Sammy recalled. "And I woke up crying, Lindsay."

"Oh Sammy, that's beautiful, why that's the neatest dream you ever---you---I----------I---Sammy! *I HAD IT TOO!*" Lindsay shout-whispered this frantically to her brother, and the two of them looked at each other wide-eyed and open-mouthed. They grabbed one another's hands and looked into each other's eyes.

"Lindsay---------what------" began Sammy.

"What's going on, Sammy?" Lindsay finished it for him. At this they just cuddled, looked at the magic ghost-place on the wall and let their imaginations run wild.

Sammy had read Sherlock Holmes, young as he was, and he had a feel for elementary logic. He stayed lost in thought for around 20 minutes, during which time his sister-pal was doing some thinking of her own and was wise enough not to distract him.

"Listen, kiddo, here's what I've been thinking," explained Sammy. "Now, we've been listening to our teachers tell us that all we're gonna learn about is state capitals and stuff. And our mom tells us we're stuck with dad's meanness forever and we can't do anything about it. And our dad tells us we're gonna be moved apart soon for our 'own good'. And we're just kids and we're supposed to listen to this stuff."

He went on, looking very serious:

"Now look at this: They all told us there are *no* ghosts. And yet, now we know different. We *couldn't* both imagine the exact same ghost at the same time! Even us 'dumb little kids' aren't *that* dumb!"

He continued, and his eyes really lit up as he said something which he'd always wanted to say, but not until the *proof* was at hand did he ever do so. And it was *now* that the proof finally *was* at hand:

"Q.T. what it means is that they're all full of beans. They're wrong. They don't know what they're talking about---and I've always known it underneath! And what *that* means it that it's up to us to forget all the baloney they've given us and find out for *ourselves* just what is the truth and what isn't! You *see?!!*"

And with that they cuddled and laughed in triumph, as though they had just solved all the problems in their lives. (Maybe they had. Who knows?)

"Oh Sammy, you genius! I'm so excited, I think I'm gonna wet my pants! What should we find out about first? Neato!"

"Elementary, my dear Watson," imitated Sammy/Sherlock. "First we sneak off to fort No. 3 and form a plan."

And they were out of their "P.J.s", into the attic, through the maze, and into fort No. 3 in a flash. It was quite warm, rather dark, and the air was ripe with mystery! They had a whole world to rediscover, now that they'd discovered that everything they'd been told was "full of beans". They sat down.

"Sammy, I'm starting to feel what you mean. We've been listening to a few people's ideas and we'd started to believe them and to be---to be---to be fenced-in by those ideas. And *they* say that we are this, can *only* do this and that, are *stuck* with that, and *can never* do this. And now we find out we can see ghosts. *Who knows* what else we really *can* do?!" Lindsay exclaimed.

*"Precisely,* Q.T., so let's start. First let's be practical and figure out what it is we really *want* to do," said Sammy, still trying to be Sherlock.

*"I* want for all meanness to end, at least around you or me," stated Lindsay.

"And *I* wish that we could be around people who didn't treat us like dumb kids---but respected us and loved us," Sammy told her.

"Yeah! Like in our dream!" Lindsay said, a bit too loudly.

"Shhhhhh," Sammy shushed her, wanting to keep their secret fort *secret.* "But you're right, our *dream* is what we want. So can we get it? I don't know. But if there can be ghosts, then there can be anything. So let's *wish* for that dream to come true. Concentrate on being there. Concentrate on the love that------"

Suddenly sweet little Lindsay began sobbing softly and she cried to her brother, still softly:

"Oh yes----oh gosh, Sammy, I want that *so* bad: so very very bad-----"

"Oh Lindsay-----*me* too----me *too!*" And at that the tears ran down Sammy's face and he grabbed his sister and held her and they cried together. They were risking opening up to their exact true feelings. The truth of what they *are* and what they *want* was now totally out in the open.

"I----I don't want to be stuck here anymore, Sammy; I want to go to where it's good, and happy," Lindsay cried to her brother, who held her even tighter.

"Me t-t-too," he cried to her, feeling just how much he really cared about all this. Even though he so often held back feelings, he wasn't now. Somehow he must find a space in this world for his real feelings. Why not here? And now?

And then the 3'x6' Persian carpet that covered the floor of fort No. 3 trembled and began to rise above the floor with them on it! It stayed hovering a couple of inches off the floor.

Lindsay and Sammy were paralyzed with fear. They sat trembling, holding each other tightly. They didn't dare move a muscle or twitch or even move their eyes.

As they hovered in mid-air, Sammy heard Lindsay breathing more and more deeply, and then she gasped and cried passionately:

"We can *DO* it, Sammy!!!" And with that they redoubled all hopes, dreams, and wishes and courage came; and they wished with all their might that they would go higher.

The carpet rose another foot. They went from afraid to rapturously delighted. They *could* do it!!!! Sammy passionately burst out:

"Higher, Lindsay, HIGHER!" And they both wished it, and it went up until their heads touched the dusty, sloped ceiling.

"Okay---*lower* now!" exclaimed Lindsay. And down it came, finally coming to a gentle landing on the attic floor. They embraced in blissful celebration of their success, laughing and breathless with hope and excitement.

Sammy must have realized that they were being too noisy, so he put his finger to his lips in a gesture of silence. He then held up 2 fingers and nodded his happy, blissful head. She nodded back.

It was a secret signal to rendezvous at fort No. 2. They'd have to sneak out against their dad's orders, but it couldn't be helped. Besides, dad was off his rocker *and* full of beans! How much more proof did they need? Lindsay rolled up the carpet and they snuck down the stairs.

Luckily, their parents' bedroom door was closed. They snuck past it, and noticed the clock's opinion of what time it was. Eight fifty-one A.M., Saturday morning. They could hear the birds' cheerful chirping and twittering. As they tip-toed slowly and ever-so-quietly down the back hall, the floor boards kept trying to creak and give them away. It was a "minefield". They were scared! They let themselves out the back door very very softly, with Lindsay carrying the precious rolled-up carpet. The door creaked faintly. They ran all the way to their camp. They pushed their way through the overlapping branches of the "secret entrance". These branches formed the "walls" of fort No. 2. They lost no time in breathlessly unrolling their vehicle. They got on and wished themselves up to about 12 feet off the ground, but the tree limbs were so plentiful and crowded up there that they couldn't go any further, so they went back down.

Sammy looked around and noticed an opening in the branches through which their carpet could probably squeeze. It was 3 feet off the ground and forward to the left. He spoke:

"Let's get up 3 feet and then get out of here, okay Q.T.?"

"Okay. Oh Sammy this is so neato---!!! I can hardly stand it!"
Lindsay was ecstatic.

"Yeah, and you know what? We're not going to run away and find what we *really* want," Sammy said, leading up to something.

"We're *not?*" And a frown started forming on the extraordinarily alive face of Lindsay.

"No. We don't need to *run* away. Now we can *FLY* away!!!" And with this she laughed and slugged him on the shoulder for teasing her.

So up they went. Three feet. And then they wished to fly away. But nothing happened. After 5 awful minutes of failure they came back down. They discussed it. He asked her if she was indeed trying to go out of the clearing. She said yes. He said he couldn't understand it---they should have gone ahead through the clearing. At this Lindsay started laughing like she'd fallen off her rocker.

Eventually Sammy got some sense out of his silly sister: She'd been trying to *back out* of the clearing through an opening she'd spotted to the *right rear!* After a good chuckle over that Sammy said:

"Okay, only one captain per ship. You be captain, O.K.? I'll be lookout and first mate. You call all the moves and I'll never argue. We've gotta work together on this one. Or we'll mess up this whole deal. Okay?"

"Got'cha, Samwich. Let's go. Let's see if I can remember from ship movies. 'All ahead full,' 'all astern half,' 'right rudder,' 'left rudder,' 'ahead slow.' Let's add some. 'Crawl ahead,' 'crawl backwards,' um---let's see---"

"Don't forget 'slope upwards' and 'slope downwards' for getting different altitudes."

"Right; okay, get on, matey." Lindsay "ordered". "All ready?"

"Ready to cast off, Captain Q.T." Sammy answered.

And up they went, and out through the front clearing they went, slick as you please.

"Steady as she goes " ordered the Captain, once they'd gotten out and were rising at about a 10-degree angle while they were also going faster and faster forward. Just as they were clearing the last of the trees a squirrel glared at them and scolded them, as if to say:

"Don't you know you don't belong up here?"

But they were tired of "shoulds" and "shouldn'ts" and they just stuck out their tongues at him.

It was a glorious day for a ride on a magic carpet. The birds were chorusing blissfully, as if enchanted; the flowers were already opened to the morning sun; the town and countryside stretched before them like a patch-work quilt. Each field was a different color. The friendly sky was robin's-egg blue and it was graced with a few fluffy cotton-ball clouds. It was perfect!

They held on real tight so they wouldn't fall off. Their hair blew furiously and their cheeks turned pink. They were tense with excitement, but not afraid. Just exhilarated. Eventually they quit thinking "faster", because it was becoming too hard to hold on.

It was chilly up high. So they went down a bit. And suddenly they realized they'd better start figuring out where they were going. They were already heading for Gateway Mountain, about 30 miles straight ahead of their carpet. So they kept the same speed and direction and were soon circling the lovely green mountain. If felt almost as if they had been led there.

As they spiralled closer and closer to the mountain, somewhat like a space-capsule approaching atmospheric re-entry, they looked for a place to land. Their hands were cramped from hanging on so long. Soon, as they travelled just above the treetops, they suddenly both thought they heard something, faintly but distinctly:

A bubbling, pretty, female laugh!

They headed for the place from which the laugh seemed to originate. But when they got there, instead of finding a person, they found an entrance to a cave.

They maneuvered into the cave slowly, and bent over to avoid bumping their heads.

It wasn't really a cave. It was a tunnel. They followed it. It went ahead and down. No matter how far they went, it went ahead and down. There was always a couple of extra feet of space over their heads. So they never bumped them.

All of a sudden Sammy said:

"Lindsay! We can *see!*"

"I always *could*, Samwich," retorted the smartypants named Lindsay.

"But there can't be sunlight down here this far. Look, Q.T., the light is coming from that green moss on the walls---isn't that weird? We can see just fine," Sammy said.

And it was true. There was luminiscent green moss everywhere. Lindsay reached up and let it brush gently through her fingertips as they hurried through the tunnel. It felt soft and spongy.

Suddenly there was a fork in the tunnel.

"Right rudder," ordered the Captain. They went on further and another fork appeared.

"Right rudder," she again ordered. So, on they travelled, down the right fork. Eventually they came to a third fork, but this one was different. *Very* different. They stopped and looked it over.

*Stared* is more like it. It couldn't possibly be, but it was. It even said so on a sign.

"Rolly Ghoster"

An eerie, hazy, luminiscent, ghostly rolly coaster stood before them, its tracks extending in each direction down the tunnel they had come to. The rolly ghoster itself was headed towards their right.

There wasn't enough clearance to fly their carpet in the narrow tunnel. So they either rode the ghoster or walked. They had a short conference and decided that they would roll up their carpet and take a chance on the ghoster.

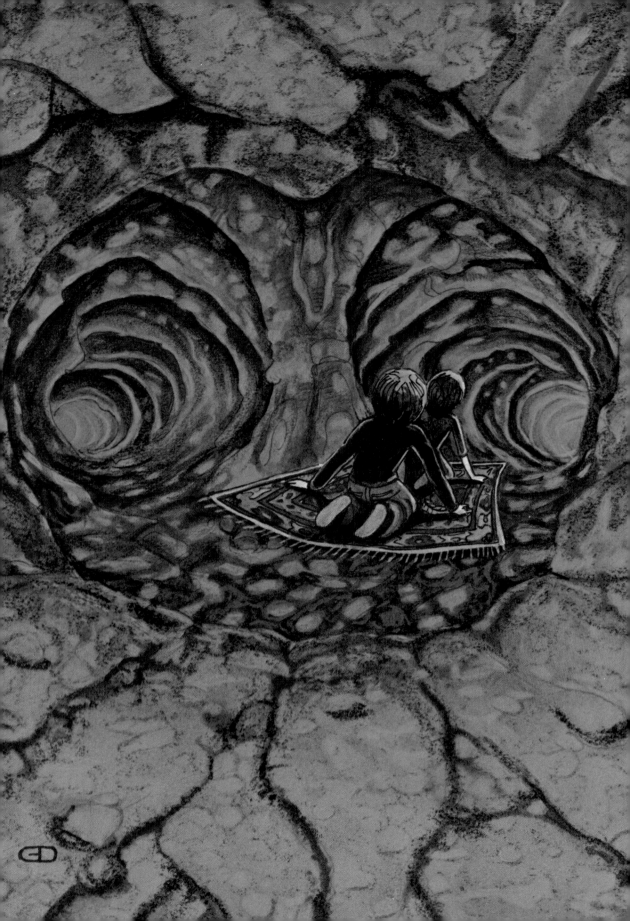

Lindsay hopped into ghoster car no. 1 and Sammy took no. 2, behind her. He carried the rug, rolled up and stuck down to where his feet were. (The other end rested against his tummy.) Their brains were churning anxiously. They were scared, but thrilled with the mysterious excitement.

They settled into the seats of the eerie ghoster, nervously. In about a minute it began to roll on its own, as if run by ghosts. Since they now knew there were ghosts, it seemed obvious to them that ghosts would be running a rolly ghoster. Off they went.

Faster and faster they shot through the narrow tunnel. It was fun at first, but it helped to close one's eyes so one didn't get ill. The tunnel was *too* narrow! The ghoster went up and down hills and around curves, but always it was in that narrow tunnel. It kept on and on, on and on, and on and on some more.

It wasn't going to stop! This terrible thought hit Lindsay first. Then it hit Sammy. Lindsay slowly turned around, looking scared and a bit ill. She looked at Sammy. He looked pale. They began to get frantic.

"What can we *do?*" screamed Lindsay.

"There's only one thing *to* do, since we only brought one thing with us. Here, grab hold," hollered Sammy. He pulled out the rolled-up carpet. Leaving it rolled up, he hoisted one end onto Lindsay's shoulder. She grabbed on and with one last brave attempt to be on top of the situation, she ordered:

"This is your captain speaking. All astern full." And they wished with all their might. There was no noticeable change in speed for a minute, but eventually they began to slow down. After what seemed like a week, they creaked eerily to a complete stop, and the weird tomblike silence of the rolly ghoster tunnels was noticed for the first time.

They hopped off quickly, before the ghoster decided to take them for another ride. They felt weak. Luckily, they were at a wide spot in the ghoster tunnel. There was room for them to lie down on their carpet and rest for a bit. Surprisingly, the ghoster stayed still as death during their "nap". Apparently it was people in the seats that made it go. Or made the ghosts make it go.

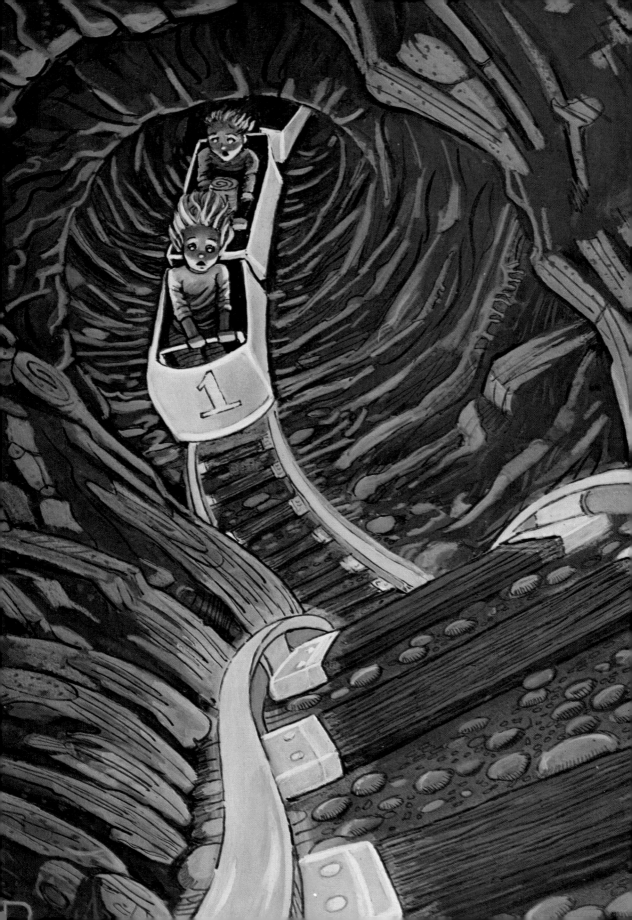

But their adventure hadn't ended yet. Not by a long shot. Lindsay shook Sammy after a bit, and though he still felt a bit shakey, he got up and they looked around. The wide part of the tunnel didn't go far, and it didn't take long to explore it.

It had only one interesting feature: there was a very small tunnel leading away from the ghoster tunnel. What else could they do?

So up the tunnel they crawled. Lindsay went first, dragging the rolled carpet behind her. Sammy brought up the rear. It must have been 2 blocks long if it was an inch. And they had acute cases of kneesus soritus once they got to the tunnel's end. (That's sutiros suseenk spelled backwards for those of you who don't speak slug latin.)

But the end of the tunnel was not a very relieving sight. It was blocked off with a board. Captain Q.T. saw her duty clearly, and she turned feet-first towards the board and stomped against it fiercely, like a battering ram.

Eventually it gave out, and to her amazement when she looked up-tunnel she discovered that there *was* no tunnel anymore. She'd kicked her way into a very eerie room! They were either in a haunted house or in a haunted room, they guessed, as they climbed out of the tunnel and into what looked like something out of Dracula's castle.

There was a big fireplace and the mantelpiece above it had many candelabra on it. All candles in these holders were lit and flickering. It was as if someone was waiting for them. But friend or foe?

The chandeliers that hung from the 25-foot-high ceiling cast a weird orange glow on the large room. The dusty, ornate oak paneling above the mantelpiece contrasted sharply with the sculptured rock of the room's other 3 walls.

Right away they heard eerie creaks and groans, which seemed to increase as time went on. It was anything but a pleasant place to visit. The very walls seemed to emit a stench of evil or danger or both.

Sammy and Lindsay stuck close together, becoming more and more nervous and hesitant. They were about ready to creep back up the tunnel from whence they came when the bubbling female laughter was heard in the direction of the paneling above the mantelpiece.

It was a lively sound, but it was terribly out of place in these surroundings. They turned towards the sound, expectantly. For a second they both saw the same thing they'd seen the night before:

A wispy, hazy, ghostlike female face, smiling at them.

"It's this way," whispered the face, which then disappeared. They approached the mantel and the panels, but there was no longer anything to see or hear.

This was all getting very confusing to our young 8-year-olds. Even the 8-year-old who read at 8th-grade level couldn't make heads or tails out of any of this.

They began to become discouraged. Just when they thought things couldn't possibly get much worse, they did. Get much worse, that is. In fact, they got *much worse* than just "much worse".

They got TERRIBLE!

Secret passageways opened at each end of the long mantel and horrid nightmare creatures came out, lurching and growling and looking hungrily, *very* hungrily, AT LINDSAY AND SAMMY!

It all happened so fast that they both screamed. They got their wits about them just long enough to each grab a long, heavy candelabrum before they ran for the opposite wall.

More creatures emerged, grunting and drooling and staggering, with rasping evil breath. Sammy and Lindsay would have begun crying for their mother or at least wishing that they were safe in their room at home, except *there was no time:* the monsters were upon them!

They knew it was life or death, and they fought valiantly and without mercy. But they were already tired when they entered the room, and more monsters kept emerging, and let's face it: 3rd graders are neither big nor strong compared to monsters. So with his arms still swinging his now-candleless candelabrum with his last bit of strength, Sammy suddenly busied his feet with kicking open and unrolling their magic carpet. It was, as always, their last hope. He called to Lindsay, and she came and they both stood upon it, now back to back, all the while fighting off the awful on-slaught of the vicious beasts. They began wishing to rise, and it was no sooner wished than done.

Soon their heads touched the 25-foot ceiling and they sat down and kept a sharp lookout on the angry ravenous creatures below, who all acted like dogs whose bones had just been snatched away.

It wasn't long before the creatures began hurling candelabra at the carpet's captain and her first mate. And again it was the captain who called out the defensive strategies.

"Ahead full! Now right rudder!" she screamed fearfully, knowing that a miscalculation on her part could spell disaster. Sammy put all his concentration into helping her wish-steer the carpet.

And as if they didn't have their hands full enough, they suddenly heard the sweet laughter again, and the ghost-face was there, in front of a high-up panel above the mantel. They didn't dare look at her, or they knew they'd be knocked off their carpet by one of the monsters' missiles. But they were able to hear her, amidst the growls and crashes and roars from below, as she suddenly addressed them:

"Lindsay-----Sammy------we all know what it is that you want more than anything else in the world. We know that you want it very very much. But do you want it badly enough to risk your life for it? Do you want it badly enough to throw away everything you've ever been told and put everything you have into reaching your goal?"

"Yes!" they replied loudly and at once.

"But how do we escape these creatures?" Sammy cried, feeling a candelabrum barely graze his left arm before it smashed into the ceiling.

"Why simply go back up the tunnel," laughed the ghost-woman. "You'll be safe then."

"But will we get what it is we want so badly then?" shouted Lindsay above the tumult below.

"No, but you'll be safe," she answered.

"But---we don't *want* to be safe by going back home," argued Sammy. "We want to live how we *really* want. Like our dream."

"Yes, I know. I *do* know how you both feel---people are like that where I come from," the ghost-lady encouraged.

"But where *do* you come from?" asked Lindsay.

"Straight behind me is a panel I'll now open (she does so). Behind that is a 6-foot-thick cement wall. Through that is a world of love and respect the likes of which you've never even dreamed about, except once."

"People are very careful about how they treat one another there. People understand each other and never hurt each other. People are neither crazy part of the time nor partly crazy all of the time. There is no selfishness or hate. We are all ONE there. And my name is Linda."

"Oh Linda---please," begged Sammy, "where is the door to your world?"

"There is none," replied Linda, and her voice was nearly drowned out by the increasing turmoil from below.

"But---you mean we can't *get* there?!" cried Lindsay desperately.

"Oh yes, my sweet friends, you CAN get there. Simply go through the cement wall," Linda encouraged.

"But---you mean---um---is there a hole or---" began Sammy.

"No hole. No door. Go through solid cement," Linda replied.

"But we *can't*, Linda!" Lindsay wailed.

"Yes, you can. But you must go as fast as you can and hit it as hard as you can and you must *believe nothing.* Do not believe you can make it. Do not believe you cannot make it. Do not believe *anything!* Simply be willing to risk finding out the truth about that wall. To do this you needn't believe or know or think, but rather *risk* and *care* and *do.*"

"But---we *can't* go through----," began Sammy.

"That's what you *believe.* Stop believing. When have you ever tried to go through a cement wall?" asked Linda.

"We haven't, but---" began Sammy.

"You see? You have no reason to believe you can or cannot do it!"

"But we've been told that---" began Lindsay.

"Told--TOLD!" Linda corrected her. "Do not believe what you hear. Beleive only what you experience for yourselves. There's only one thing standing between you 2 kids and the world of love you've wanted since the day you were born--*beliefs!* I must go now. But one last question will be in order before I go:

Do Carpets *Fly?"*

And with this, the most beautiful and loving and sweet and compassionate look that either child had ever even imagined came over the face of the angelic Linda, whose face became more and more hazy, and finally disappeared.

They narrowly missed being upset by the next hurled object---the creatures were getting desperate.

The children were exhausted and their heads were spinning: Would they risk their lives and go full-speed into that wall, or go back up the tunnel and end up at home?

"Well, what do you say, Sammy?" asked Lindsay, halfway between desperation and exhilaration.

"I say we go for it. It's easy to see that there's never going to be an easy way to get our ticket to that world. But I say it's worth the risk. How about you?"

There was a 10-second pause.

"This is your captain speaking. We shall now build up ramming speed. All ahead full and keep circling until we are full speed. Then hit the wall---HARD!!" ordered Lindsay.

"Aye aye, captain!" shouted Sammy, and they began to circle. As they circled faster and faster they remembered Linda's words: "Do carpets fly?" If carpets fly and the school and their dad and everyone else were full of beans, and ghosts really exist, then a "belief" that no one can get through a cement wall is simply a lot of "beans", just like everything else they'd been told. Onward!

When full speed had been reached they hurled straight into the cement wall, after a "Now!" from the captain. They charged through it, *risking everything and believing nothing.*

There was a blinding flash and suddenly they came shooting out of the side of a hill of rock and into a clear, cool, moonlit night. They were hurling upward and forward at a frightening rate.

It had been daytime when they left their world, but here in the new world it was night.

They both thought "full astern" as fast and as hard as possible, and slowed down their craft before it smashed against some tree or other obstacle.

"We *did* it, Sammy!" Lindsay shrieked happily, hugging her brother, sighing and beginning to cry all at once.

She sure cried a lot lately!

They were both happy beyond all words. They cruised along at a safe speed. They floated timelessly. They'd left their beliefs behind. The world expanded before them. It was so beautiful, so perfect---life felt incredibly full and deep, sweet and inspiring. It was as if a curtain had been opened and they saw the underlying beauty in everything. Everything was so clear, so bright, so---good and lovable. Things didn't seem separate anymore---no matter where they looked or what they saw, it all seemed to be part of one big ALL.

It was like falling in love with life. It was like coming Home.

Suddenly they heard the beautiful laughter again in the distance. It seemed to call to them. It seemed to be calling them home.

Just as suddenly, millions of glitterbugs in front of them began to emit sparkling trails of golden rain---rain like the rain their lovely dream had dissolved into only last night. The multi-colored comet-tails glittered and twinkled irresistibly, marking a trail ahead of Lindsay and Sammy that was impossible to miss. Showers of sparkling lights, leading to the land of love.

It was all too beautiful. It must be a dream. Could all this *really* be real?

A whole squadron of glitterbugs converged upon the carpet and led them in a breathtaking shower of golden and silver rain. Breathlessly they flew to the next clearing, where their new life was waiting. They wished their carpet down; it landed, and they stood up and turned around, their hearts overflowing with happy excited feelings.

Strange, but beautiful and fantastic, was the way everything looked to Sammy and Lindsay. The houses were large, round, smooth, full of curves, and felt warm and inviting. There were no corners or angles---everything just sort of flowed into everything else . . . as if these dwellings had GROWN there. The trees and bushes were all so strange and fantastic---and yet *terribly beautiful.*

They saw a figure approach. A beautiful white-robed woman with a glorious aura about her approached them with her arms opened wide. They knew her now. They ran forward crying happily, forward and into the loving arms of the beautiful Linda, who was now no longer a ghost, but a warm, touchable, sweet human being!


All was joy, all was tenderness. They'd been promised a new life and a new home and love, with no hate or selfishness, and that is what they got. They kept pinching themselves to see if they'd wake up from this wonderful dream. But they never did.

In this world there were always dozens of moms and dads for any kid to choose from when he or she needed affection or understanding. No one was ever "stuck with" anyone. (Not that there were mean or hateful people to avoid like in the other world---there weren't).

It was *very important* here that every kid got to *choose* who he or she would be around.

And kids always got plenty of space to be alone and do their thing, with no one bothering them.

At school kids got to find out and learn about what they were interested in, not what *others* thought they "should" know. And they got lots of opportunities to learn by *experience* at school, not by an unending stream of *words,* like in their old school.

Lindsay and Sammy were so happy that they could hardly stand it.

There was one very very surprising thing that they found out about love in the new world. In fact, they were beginning to suspect that maybe what they'd learned about love applied to all worlds and all people, everywhere. Here is what happened:

For a few days the 2 new love-children were seeking out and receiving love from just about everyone. And they *always* got it. Everyone was honestly extremely fond of Sammy and Lindsay and loved expressing it.

But then a strange thing happened. They got *full* of love. All of a sudden they had all the love they *needed*. Which let them desire being loved, and appreciate being loved, but for the first time in their lives, *not need any more love.*

Curiouser and curiouser it became, because their *focus* changed: they quit being concerned about themselves and what *they* could get, and how much love they could get---and suddenly began thinking about other people besides themselves. Suddenly here were a couple of 8-year-old kids who actually became genuinely interested in how much love *others* were getting, and whether *other* people were happy.

And they weren't doing this out of gratitude, like in a bargain when you pay someone back who has done something for you. No---it was real, natural, genuine, inner interest on their part. It was the way things naturally developed. And no one in the new world was surprised, because apparently it happened to all the people who ever came to their world from other worlds.

They had come wanting and needing everything. But in no time they felt full and secure about all needs being fulfilled, and so they became interested in other people.

So *that's* what Linda had meant in the haunted room when she told them that where she came from people are very concerned with how they treat each other. It was true! They were! It just came about naturally. Everyone listened, cared, and understood you.

People were especially understanding and nice about *feelings*. They expressed their exact true feelings around each other, so no one had to lie or hide or pretend. So no one was ever nervous, hostile, or suspicious, much less guilty, scared or hateful. Everyone was happy. It was amazing!

So *that's* why Linda had guided them to her world by the use of happy, bubbling, loving, sweet laughter! It was truly the way she *felt* about life! It *was* Linda!

$\mathfrak{E}$ventually there came a time when Lindsay and Sammy began wishing to let their parents and friends know they were all right. They also wished to see if any of their old friends or if even their parents wanted to come and join them here in the new world.

What?! Bring their mean father *here?!* Well, you see, they no longer *needed* him, so they didn't have to stay mad at him anymore. It was now really *okay* with them if he didn't love them. Simply because they didn't *need* it from him anymore.

Linda smiled gently as the 2 children talked over some of these desires with her. It was as if she already knew what the result would be of a trip back to the old world. But she was quite willing to give them the chance to find out for themselves. That's called giving someone "space". It's the space to find out for oneself.

She could have *told* them what the result would be, but by doing that she'd merely give them words to be "believed" and they'd "believe" them, but they'd be as far away from the truth about going back as they ever were. The truth comes from *experience*. Like the way they found out about the 6-foot-thick cement wall!

They'd been in the new world for only 6 weeks. Naturally within the first few days of arriving at their new home they'd asked a million questions. A lot of strange things had been happening in their lives. And the questions *were* answered. (If *you* find *yourself* bursting with such questions, you can turn to "Details" at the end of this story. But if you can wait a bit, the story is nearly over, so you'll get your questions answered soon anyway.)

So Lindsay and Sammy prepared for a visit back home. They were ready by nightfall, but decided to get a good sleep and set off on their visit early the next morning.

Soon after takeoff, the adventurous Captain Lindsay and her First Mate Sammy were heading straight for the side of a mountain. They weren't going too fast, or they'd end up smashing into the far side of the room in their old world.

Sammy looked at Lindsay nervously. They already knew they'd be able to get through, but would they be able to start circling fast enough, once inside, to avoid hitting the far wall?

They were hanging on real tight. Closer and closer they came---they were nearly to it---now! There was a flash of light and they both thought "circle" as hard as they possibly could.

From another universe, Linda was putting her all into a telepathic assist, making sure they had such a high level of control over their carpet that they'd get it circling in time.

They made it! They circled slower and slower and came to rest near the tunnel. The kids lost no time in rolling up their "craft" and crawling into that tunnel. They didn't want to tangle with any "creatures" again.

They reached the rolly ghoster and rode it for about a minute. They made it stop near a 6-foot-tall tunnel entrance. They entered it, unrolled the carpet, and the journey continued.

After a nice flight through the eerie green tunnel, they found a fork, and then another fork, and finally they saw daylight ahead!

Out they flew, and up they went, picking up more and more speed. They leveled off at what was probably 800 feet or so and zoomed along as nice as you please, having a wonderful time being in such total *control* of their destination, their carpet, and their lives. The flight was exhilarating. It had been early morning in the other world, but it was sunset in their old world.

It was near the end of June and very warm. The sunset with its delicate pink and orange light framing the mountains on the western horizon was gorgeous as they viewed it from their carpet. Their view of the countryside was breathtakingly lovely. They felt like staying up there forever, flying around.

They got to the woods that bordered their little town just as the last trace of pink vanished from the west. It was nearly dark. Down they went, and soon they were just clearing the treetops. They slowed way down and headed for the park in which fort No. 2 was hidden. Then they poked their carpet through the 3-foot-high opening and entered their fort.

Discussion began about "how to proceed". They needed a plan.

"You know we're gonna get a lickin' from dad, don't you?" Sammy asked Lindsay.

"Yeah, I suppose---but I guess I still want to visit them, at least this one last time. Gosh, Sammy, doesn't it feel *weird* to not feel like we *need* anything from anyone around here?" asked Lindsay.

"Yeah, it sure does. Well---I guess I can take one more lickin' if I have to. I really wanna give them a chance to find out that things don't have to always be the way they are here. How about you?" asked Sammy.

"Yup. So what's the plan?" asked Lindsay.

"Well, first let's hide the carpet here under some leaves, where no one can take it away from us. Then let's figure out about how we're gonna tell Georgie or Frankie or---

"Or Sylvia or Karen or Dish-Water or Josie," put in Lindsay. "I say we raid our piggybank and use our money to call from a phone booth where we won't get messed with. Remember how dad picked on you the last time you were calling--"

"Don't remind me," responded Sammy. "But you're right. That's a neat plan, Captain Q.T." He gave her an affectionate hug, and she hugged back and told Sammy:

"You're the best brother in the world, Samwich."

"And you're the neatest sister. Gee, it seems so strange to be back here, where there is so much misery and---and needing--you know, everyone needs everything and--and everyone---and--and stuff. *You* know," Sammy told her. "Well---let's see what happens."

They were first hugged and squeezed, and their parents made a fuss over them. But it wasn't long before their father was "teaching them to never run away again", and that meant spankings.

He hollered at them about all the trouble and problems their running away had caused him. He let them know how ashamed they should be for "treating him like that". He made them "promise not to do it again", although it never even occured to them to keep such a crazy promise. And then he made them tell where they'd been.

But when he heard them start talking about carpets, tunnels, ghosts, and universes, he just gave them an ugly look and told them he'd give them "one more chance".

So why get more spankings? They made up a dumb story about a farmer picking them up and letting them work at his farm and play with his animals. Their father was satisfied, but they were sent to their room with no supper.

"Things sure don't change much around here, do they?" Lindsay said to her brother.

But Sammy was pondering something very interesting: they hadn't shed any tears during their spankings! It had hurt in a different way. Apparently the tears they used to shed over spankings were about the understanding and tenderness they *didn't* receive---not about the sore rear-ends they *did* receive.

And up she came, right on schedule, to apologize for what "dad did", ---or was it for what *she didn't* do? Like make him quit beating his kids, for instance. But they still loved her, and they missed her (though they felt that they didn't *need* her). They overlooked her nonsense and just hugged her and enjoyed it, without thinking.

They told her the whole true story of where they'd been. And, of course, she didn't believe them. She said it was a wonderful story, though, and someday they would probably grow up to be story book writers.

Sammy and Lindsay felt weirdly calm----like they knew before they even told her that mom wouldn't believe their story. So----

Sammy went out, night or not, and fetched the carpet and brought it back. He unrolled it, got on with his sister, and together they made it rise and fly around the room.

Their mom looked up at them wide-eyed and Lindsay asked her, still flying:

*"Now* do you believe us?"

Mother looked frightened and got them to bring it down. And then she proceeded to talk to them seriously, acting as if the whole deal with the carpet had never really happened.

She let them know that she couldn't possibly believe their story because she'd learned, in her 38 years of life, that *people are not really like that.* She was talking about all the love, beauty, tenderness, and lack of any hate, fear, guilt, selfishness, lying or pretending that the kids had just told her about---about the "way it was" where they'd been. Mother went on:

"You see, the devil lurks in all of us. There will *never* be people or places like you told me about, because people are basically evil. Why do you think there are policemen, lawyers, judges, and priests? Why do you suppose there are so many many laws, and churches? To keep people in line! To keep people from slipping back into their underlying nature, which is evil. And sinful. One must forget the trials and tribulations of today and begin preparing one's path for the final day of judgment. One must prepare to be *saved!* One must-------------"

"Mom?" Sammy asked gently of his mother, whom he hadn't been listening to. He'd heard this type of stuff before. It was *words.* But he *had* caught "One must prepare to be *saved!*"

"Yes, dear?" Mother calmed down a bit. Sammy put his arms around his mother and looked up into her eyes. Tears began to form in his eyes and soon they were running down his face.

"Mom", he said gently. "We *are* saved, and---and we wanted to see if ------if-----if you would come too." The tears came fast, and his mother's image blurred. Then Lindsay came over and hugged her too, crying, and sobbing:

"Mom! It's true----we really *did!* We want you to have a chance too! Honest!"

At this their mother began weeping. It was the first time she'd felt loved in so long that she couldn't even remember *how* long. Eventually she told them, still crying:

"Thanks so much, kids---thanks so much for caring---" and then she left them, looking very happy and sad at the same time.

Neither said a word. They looked into each other's eyes---both knew what the other was feeling. There was no need for words---no need at all.

They went to bed. Long minutes went by. As Sammy was beginning to get sleepy he heard a whisper from his sister's bed:

"Sammy?" Lindsay called, softly.

"Hmmm?" he replied, softly.

"Sammy----I love you." she whispered.

There was a short silence.

"I know, honey---I love you too," Sammy whispered. They had never said anything like that before. They'd felt affectionate before and had kidded each other about it. But neither had ever used the word "love" or "honey". What 8-year-olds did? And yet now they were no longer regular 8-year-olds.

The sudden feeling of their own mother needing them more than they needed her was incredible to Sammy and Lindsay. They each felt like *her loving mother* when they tried to get her to come with them! It had also made them realize how they didn't "need" *each other* any longer. There were oodles of wonderful, loving, fun kids and adults to be with back in their real home.

They knew they'd be around each other lots because of how fond they were of each other. But no longer would they be forced together out of need. Now it was simply liking each other that would bring them together. She loved what was in his heart, and he loved what was in her heart. It was beautiful. But it wasn't *need*. It was a mind-blower of a realization.

Their parents had never gotten to the place where they didn't *need* something from the people they were with, nor had their friends. Sammy and Lindsay had. And they were just now finding out what an entirely different universe that made it. It took coming back to their *old* universe to see this completely.

As they dozed off they kept hearing far-off, lovely, bubbly laughter.

There wasn't really much to do when they woke up. They already knew what would happen. But they wanted to try. It was Saturday, luckily, so that meant that their friends would be glued to their T.V.'s. They broke their piggy bank and snuck out to a phone booth. They needed *space* . . . so they could talk without parents around.

During the phonecalls their friends merely laughed at them. And after 2 calls Sammy convinced Lindsay that they would do more good if they tried merely to give their friends a better chance for the *future*. So they wrote a letter on a tablet they'd bought, copied it 8 times, signed them all, bought stamps and envelopes, and sent them to all their friends.

The letters were brief and to the point, and went like this:

"Dear _____,
    Your feelings are your best guide--follow them and don't lose them.
    Don't believe what you are told--believe only your feelings.
Find out for *yourself* what is true---and what is real.
    A world of love waits for those who are ready to risk everything, be brave, and believe nothing. Listen for the call.
    There *are* ghosts. There *are* magic carpets. And there *is* a world of beauty. But don't *believe* us. Instead, just keep listening for the call. NEVER GIVE UP!
                                Love,
                                Sammy and Lindsay"

They went home, somehow managing to sneak upstairs and then come noisily back down, pretending that they had just gotten up.

The sweet fragrance of blueberry waffles filled the kitchen. Mom was making their favorite breakfast. It was as if in some part of her heart she knew that she was never going to see her children again. They sat down at the table and ate hungrily, even though tears kept trying to form in the corners of their eyes. The waffles were sweet and crisp and the applesauce mom served with them added the perfect extra touch.

After breakfast, the love-children went up and got on very warm jackets and sweaters. They planned to have one last tour of this world, and they wanted it to be a high and exciting one. And that meant it would be a chilly one.

After they came down, they went up to their dad and hugged him and said goodbye. He asked them where they were going. They said "outside", which was true. It was said with such self-assurance and maturity that he forgot that they were "supposed" to be "grounded".

He couldn't understand why there was such a strange and sweet and happy look in each of their faces. Anyway he said "g'bye", just to humor them. They hugged their mother then, and went out.

Sammy had snuck the carpet into the garage. He walked over, picked it up and carried it to a spot outside the kitchen window. Inside were his parents, drinking coffee and talking.

Sammy and Lindsay got on the carpet and thought "up". It went, but they stopped it once it was even with the window. Lindsay hollered to their father:

"Ask mom where we're going---she knows. 'Bye dad. We love you."
And then Sammy shouted to their mom:

"Bye mom. We love you too."

Their parents were dumbstruck. They'd heard and understood it all, but they didn't know what to do about it. So they stared. And then they saw their children flying away on a flying carpet, waving lovingly.

Their children loved them, but their children were leaving them. They were going away on a flying carpet. Now the looks they'd seen earlier on their kids' faces made sense.

It was *really* GOODBYE!

Mr. and Mrs. Jones sat paralyzed looking at a tiny receding speck in the sky. These kids had had nowhere else to go but *them* whenever their sweet little hearts felt need---

These children had eventually turned to each other for warmth.

These children now knew where to go and what to do to find a whole new universe full of love.

They were no longer "dumb kids waiting for someone to tell them what to do next."

They were love-children, flying into the horizon, flying higher and still higher, towards the loving warmth of the sun.

"Where did we go wrong?" Mrs. Jones whispered to herself, shaking her head sadly. She began to cry softly.

### THE END

# DETAILS

The following details were not necessary to this story, so they were left out.

But as a young person grows older and perhaps wishes to delve deeper into some of life's most intriguing mysteries, he or she may find the following details capable of significantly enriching the relevancy, meaning, and context of THE MAGIC CARPET AND THE CEMENT WALL.

Dear Reader,

Hello again. I'm Linda. Richard asked me if I would mind explaining my world to you; and its relation to your world. I'd be delighted. Let's see if we can have some fun with this:

First of all, the relationship between our 2 different worlds is called PARA-LLEL UNIVERSES. These are worlds that are "next to" each other but you can't see, detect, find out about, or get from one to the other. There's a tremendous problem about getting from one to another, a problem so difficult that even your Einstein wouldn't have been much help with it.

To be honest, I don't understand these parallel universes at all, nor does anyone else. But I CAN tell you about how we or Sammy or Lindsay (or perhaps you, some day) go from one to another.

You see, you CANNOT go from one to another. Well, now you think I'm off my rocker, because I just told you that I'd tell you how one goes from one to another. But what I really meant is not "how one gets from one to another", but "how one gets from one to another to another". I suppose that sounds even crazier yet. Let's see if I can make it simpler.

Take my word for it: NO ONE knows how to draw an accurate picture of these universes or the way they're related. But let's PRETEND we can, okay?

Let this be the first one. Call it universe No. 1:

Let this be the second one, parallel to the first. Let's call it universe No. 2:

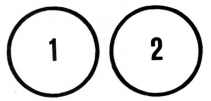

Now let's say that the "rules" are that since you must always be in SOME universe SOMEwhere (or you wouldn't exist) then that means that in all diagrams you must be (whether moving about or not) inside a closed line, which in the above case means within a circle.

Now, let's suppose that we put in 2 parallel lines to represent the relationship of the position of one universe to the position of the other:

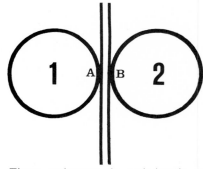

These universes do not touch each other but "are 6 feet apart", and the reason it is impossible to travel from one to the other is that in between "A" and "B" on the picture you'd be in NO universe, which is impossible.

So it's like that "Maine-joke" (which Richard told me about) where the tourist asks directions to a specific place and the old-timer hems and haws and falters and finally ends up saying:

"Nope, ye kayn't git theya from heya."

Anyway, if you're done laughing at that, we'll go on. Suppose we can enclose the space between A and B somehow so that one would be SOMEWHERE in between universes, and therefore it would be possible to go from universe No. 1 to universe No. 2.

Let's put our cement wall in between the 2 universes:

So if our cement wall can meet the qualifications of being SOMEWHERE, then suddenly there IS one place in each world where one can travel between universes.

Remember that there are 3 spacial dimensions and one time dimension in our normal universes. Horizontal, vertical, and depth could represent the SPACE dimensions. Think of a box:

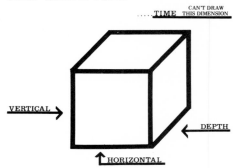

CAN'T DRAW
..... TIME  THIS DIMENSION

VERTICAL

DEPTH

HORIZONTAL

But if you try to conceptualize a 4th dimension on that box (to call time) you'll go nuts---it's not easy to picture, is it?

So if 4-dimensional time/space is what's in our normal universes, then it must be something ELSE that our cement wall is made up of.

So let's call the wall, the monsters that came out of it (since they surely don't come from MY world!), and the entire universe they exist in A 7-DIMENSIONAL UNIVERSE WITH 7-DIMENSIONAL MATTER ("matter" would include the wall and the creatures) AND 7-DIMENSIONAL TIME/SPACE. Okay? Seven's as good a number as any.

But you say: "that cement wall sounds like ordinary 4-dimensional matter to me."

Well, remember those kids going THROUGH it? They couldn't go through just ANY matter. Just 7-dimensional matter. Why? Because that matter was from a different dimension, and the physical and atomic laws of one dimension often don't apply to another dimension. Matter from 4th dimensional time/space could go through matter in 7th dimensional time/space as if it weren't really there. But not ALL of the matter from 4th dimensional time/space could do this. Only special matter could. Only matter with energy of especially high quality.

Let's call one of the basic forces that holds matter together ELECTRO-STATICS. Let's say that there are many aspects of electrostatic forces. For our purposes, we'll call 3 of the main aspects of electrostatic forces x-force, y-force, and z-force. Let's further assert that neither x-forces nor y-forces of matter from our dimension have any effect upon matter from 7-dimensional time/space.

But z-forces DO affect 7-dimensional matter. And if our matter began affecting "their" matter at times like the time Sammy and Lindsay were penetrating the wall, then they would have smacked into the wall rather than penetrating it. That's because cumulative electrostatic forces are very POWERFUL.

It's difficult to conceptualize a situation in which PARTICLES of either type of matter can freely interpenetrate each other with no effect even though the FORCES of one dimension's matter DO pull on the matter of the other dimension. Yes, even though the matter of their dimension can never totally exist in this dimension (but remains ethereal and nebulous and unreal in relation to it), that single aspect (z) of 4-dimensional matter's electrostatic FORCES does have a concrete and definite effect on 7-dimensional matter.

This effect is not one that would cause our MATTER to collide with theirs; no, the effect is more like this type of an effect:

## THEORETICAL MODEL

(Ignore the fact that in reality the little magnet would probably flip over in flight and stick to the big one)

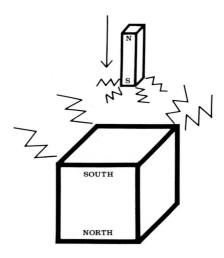

Imagine a small but very powerful magnet dropping rapidly towards a huge and tremendously powerful magnet. Let's say that the poles are lined up so that similar poles (both "south") will soon be colliding. (Like poles repel each other, unlike poles attract each other.) What will happen?

Well, the force of gravity is strong, but not as strong as the strengths of the magnetic fields these magnets have. A tiny distance before the magnets collide, the repulsive force of "like" poles of such strong magnetic fields becomes so intense (due to proximity) that it overcomes the force of gravity totally (as well as the stored kinetic energies of the falling, inertia-laden magnet), and the big magnet repels the little one---by bouncing it back up into the air, without either magnet having touched the other! (To see how this situation works, get 2 ring-shaped magnets from a hobby store, radio supply store, or scientific catalogue. Have like poles facing one another, and then drop one on the other, with a pencil through them as a "steadier". The top one bounces away from the bottom one and hovers in air magically, without ever having touched the bottom magnet---if they're strong enough.)

## EXPERIMENTAL MODEL
(try it, you'll like it)

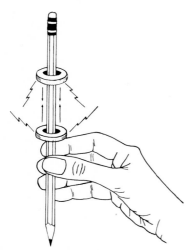

# 7-DIMENSIONAL ENERGY FIELD

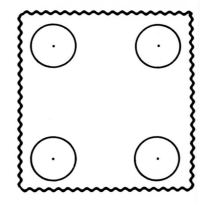

So you can see that the collision of "matter with matter" need never happen, in order for a collision or at least ALL THE EFFECTS OF A COLLISION to occur. All that is required is a collision of forces. The matter (Sammy, Lindsay, and the carpet) would attempt to "make it through", but the z-force aspect of their matter's electrostatic forces would slam against the 7-dimensional matter and that would be the end of that.

But they DID make it through! Yes, and the reason is that their z-force had been neutralized by the anti-z-force side-effect of their high quality energy. You see, as it happens: the higher the energy quality of matter from 4-dimensional time/space, the more neutralized the z-aspect of this matter's electrostatic forces becomes.

So the high-quality aspects of the energy of Sammy, Lindsay, and their carpet during their wall-penetration episode was their ticket to make it through. More pictures:

4-dimensional matter's z-force slams into cement wall of the 7-dimensional universe:

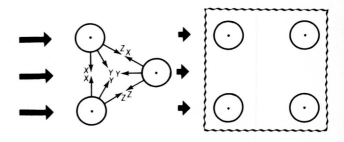

4-dimensional matter:

## ATTRACTIVE FORCES

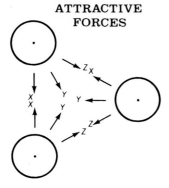

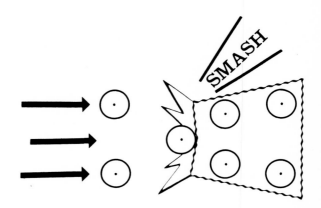

But 4-dimensional matter whose energy
has been raised to high quality by brav-
ery, telekinetics, lifewish, etc., no longer
affects 7-dimensional matter:

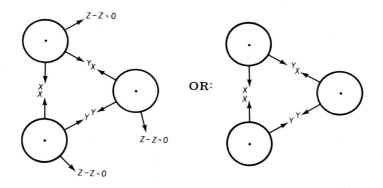

So 4-dimensional matter interpenetrates
freely with 7-dimensional:

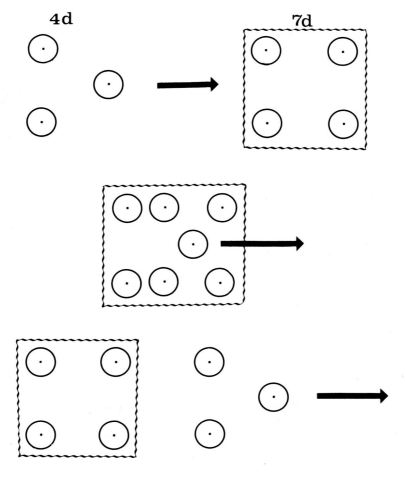

Now, to go on: it "looks like" the monsters' universe is 6 feet thick. But it's not. It just looks that way to US. To the creatures, they merely walked through their world's matter (which 7-dimensional creatures do all the time) and came out in your world and tried for a quick snack. Do you remember that they opened panels to get to the kids? THEY can't walk through 4-dimensional panels (because of the z-forces in the panels) any more than we can. These panels are just outside the wall in that 7-dimensional universe.

The REASON the creatures came is: sound. The kids talked and the sound waves easily passed through different universes, since sound is merely a vibration of matter that gets passed along. It's not matter itself. The creatures heard the kids and came running.

How can it look TO US (who are drawing these diagrams or looking at them) as though the 7-dimensional universe is 6' thick if it's NOT? Well, like I've already said, what we're drawing CAN'T BE DRAWN! To illustrate the paradox, let's look at where you REALLY are in the diagrams:

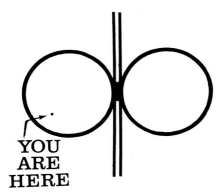

YOU
ARE
HERE

From your perspective, universe No. 2 is invisible, because it's behind a "nowhere"-barrier, and the 7-dimensional universe is simply non-tangent to our universe, except at the cement wall, so it's behind a nowhere-barrier also. But if you COULD see it, it'd be a universe that extended forever in every direction when you were facing the direction of its tangency to our universe. (More on tangency later.) In NO WAY would it look thin, plate-like, or 6' thick.

So you see how these drawings give you an impossible perspective (a "from-nowhere" viewpoint) of what's really there? The "flat" shape we see now is analogous to a mirage. Even universe No. 2 people would see the monsters' universe as infinite, from their perspective.

Now, in normal universes, gravity's effect on light creates a finite visible universe that is like a closed line forming a bounded space. But in 7-dimensional universes, gravity works so differently (including failing to bend light and therefore failing to create a closed-lined, bounded, finite, limited space) that our 4-dimensional matter would perceive itself to be in a situation of being NOWHERE if it were anywhere (except in the closed-space cement wall or something equally as bounded) in that universe.

Anyway, now you can see what force is behind the impossiblity of using anything that's not solid to serve as a door between universes No. 1 and No. 2. It's gravity, or more specifically, gravity's failure to create a bounded space by bending 7th dimensional light photon's paths.

So what about the carpet? Well, ordinarily it would have been of low quality energy and couldn't have made it, but telekinetic vibrations and telekinetic assist vibrations are of high-quality energy, and neutralized the z-force in the carpet's matter. Let me explain:

The kids used their minds to make the carpet move, which is called telekinesis. I transmitted, mentally, a telekinetic assist vibration, which amplified their mind's attempts and made the carpet's matter more receptive to their telekinetic vibrations. You've probably already heard of Uri Geller moving or bending things with his mind on T.V., so you aren't too surprised at this.

But he only moves small things. The kids would also have been limited to moving small things except that I sent along an assist. If "9" means "move a small thing" and both the kids AND I were emitting "9"-type vibrations, and any number over 50 means "move a big thing" and their force was being multiplied by mine (my assist), then 9x9=81, or "move a very big thing relatively slowly", like the ghoster, or "move an average-sized thing very fast", like the carpet. You see?

Incidentally, the kids' clothes made it through because of a process called high level energy INDUCTION. Anything a fraction of an inch from high-quality energized matter (the kids) became affected by the high-quality energy-field around it, and got induced with enough high-quality energy to make it through. However, the kids couldn't bring any of their possessions back to the new world. Not unless they were like clothes and could be within their "field". Fortunately they'd lost interest in "possessions" anyway.

But let's get to something more basic. Lindsay and Sammy are kids who were at the crisis point---they cared as much as it's possible to care about whether they really got to live or whether they simply had to give up their real feelings for good. Not only is that high-quality energy (or just call it "life-wish" if you like), but it's also the easiest type of energy to pick up, telepathically.

TELEPATHY is mind-to-mind communication through psychic energies alone. I have been chosen as the one, of all the people in my world, to telepathically tune in on the people in your world to see when someone cares with such high lifewish energy that he or she could surely reach the high-quality energy-level needed to pass through the cement wall.

WHY I was chosen is simple: I am the best at it of anyone we know of. So when I pick up on someone who cares as Sammy and Lindsay did, and still do, I contact them and send out "the call", and lead them here.

In CONTACTING them I tune in on what they really really deeply want, and then at night I project that feeling onto their dream screen. Another picture:

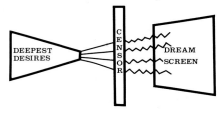

When their deepest desires get felt in dreams, normally, they have to go through a "censor" which is a translucent filter which boggles up the images until their dreams no longer clearly show their deepest desires.

However, here is the picture when I help them get to the TRUTH!:

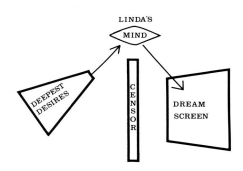

I pick up their deepest desires, which can be found in their psychic vibrations by anyone as sensitive to them as myself, and I telepathically project them down onto their dream screens. You see how I snuck past their "censors"? This is analogous to the way a T.V. station will use orbiting satellites to bounce their programs off of, if they wish to avoid interference from a high mountain range.

These desires are usually censored, because if the dreamers could feel what they really really want and need all the time, they'd soon go crazy from the pain of feeling all those needs but not having them get filled.

But what I do is to let them know their own truths, their own needs and desires, no matter how painful. And then instead of watching them "go crazy", I send out "the call" which leads them to my world where they will no longer have

to BE in pain, because those needs will ALL be filled completely, with much joy and respect and happiness.

THE CALL results in and contributes to a way (carpet telekinesis) for them to use and direct all the energy that's released when they finally get into the full feelings of what they really really want. Once traveling begins, following the call is mostly just a matter of following the sound of my laughter, which leads them to my world. But BEFORE they run away to seek what they really want, the call comes in a ghostly form. At least YOU call it that.

I call it ASTRAL PROJECTION. I transfer an image of myself to the vicinity of the child in question. This is one very strong step in the direction of encouraging kids to let go of their beliefs (which are the lowest quality energy) and go by what they experience only (which is potentially the highest quality energy). Whatever adults of that world don't understand they call "impossible", and they spread "beliefs" about it, especially to children. Once I destroy the credibility of all this nonsense that the adults have put into their kids' heads, I give the kids space to open up their feelings and minds to LIFE, not to the words and beliefs of others.

More basics, now. While the people in your world are busy fighting wars and building bigger and better machines and computers, and trying to get rich and accumulate possessions and prestige, the people in my world are (and have been for tens of thousands of Earth-years) evolving their hearts, their minds, their psychic powers, their societal structures, and their understanding.

Your world would be much happier if it followed that path too, but since it doesn't, all we can do is invite those who care enough (to be able to drop beliefs enough to get through the cement wall) to come and live and love with us.

And that means CHILDREN! Adults would rather die than drop their beliefs! But there's another reason why we "call" children only. Even if adults could get through the wall, it would do them no good at all, the way our world is set up.

You see, by the time a person in your world is anywhere from 5 to 10 years of age (occasionally much earlier or later) he/she reaches a crisis at which point it's too painful to keep feeling his/her true feelings and needs, so he/she gives up and becomes basically UNREAL. From that point on "love" is nice, makes a good environment, and feels nice, but it doesn't get "through". To get it "through" you first must get that person "turned back on" again.

To enable a person to get a chance to be nurtured and happy through REALLY RECEIVING love, it is important that he/she must not yet have reached "the crisis" (at which point he/she decides to turn off and give up, to avoid further pain). Love will nurture and be fully received by a person who hasn't reached the crisis. The person will be open to it, since he/she hasn't yet turned off his/her real feelings.

If the person is past his/her turn-off/give-up point, then he/she will need such help as "Primal Therapy" (to eliminate pain that is keeping him/her turned off) until the point is reached where he/she can turn back on again. Only at this point will his/her response to love lead to a fully nurtured, open, beautiful life like in my world.

But we are not equipped to do "therapy" here, nor do we want to. So we send the call to not-yet-turned-off people only. Another picture:

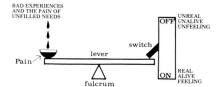

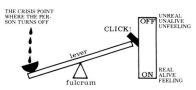

But it really doesn't matter at all whether we'd like to be "therapists" here or not. ALL such turned-off people would be unable to drop enough beliefs to get through that wall. You see, like "pain", "beliefs" are very hard to let go of.

Anyone holding on to enough pain to be past the give-up point, and basically unreal, would no longer be able to give up many beliefs, because his/her life would now be ABOUT beliefs. Not about FEELINGS, the way ALIVE people's lives are.

Next question: Who built the rolly ghoster? Well, we of my world did. The many tunnels before the ghoster all eventually lead to the ghoster, and the many smaller tunnels that lead away from different wide spots in the ghoster tunnel all eventually lead to the haunted room adjacent to the cement wall. And the reason we built the ghoster is as a test of courage, desire, will, and life-wish. There are plenty of opportunities to give-up. And if you're the give-up type, you'd never make it through the wall anyway.

So if we made that wall TOO accessible and give-up types could reach it, then there'd be a lot of people dying trying to get through that wall. The creatures would LOVE the free meals, but the people certainly wouldn't like BEING those free meals!

There have been and are (on my world) teams of telepathic-assist people who wear signal-bracelets that detect the presence of people on the ghoster-seats and signal the wearers to begin their assists. These assists make the entire ghoster controllable by the telekinetic efforts of one child (so they hadn't needed to use their carpet at all, in stopping the ghoster).

Psychic energies (like most other energies), as you can see, pass through the different-dimensional types of matter with no difficulty. That's because psychic energy and high-quality 4-dimensional energy are compatible with all forms and dimensions of matter. However, even after all these thousands of years of psychic development, we STILL have no idea WHAT "psychic energy" really IS!

The glitterbugs were trained by us to respond to psychic signals from our people by emitting their beautiful golden showers of light. We signal them to lead wall-penetrators to our settlements once we pick up the vibes that they got through.

The reason (at least part of it) the creatures of the 7-dimensional universe don't enter the world of my people and cause grief is that we have the area outside our side of the wall fenced off with high electrical fences. Here's a picture:

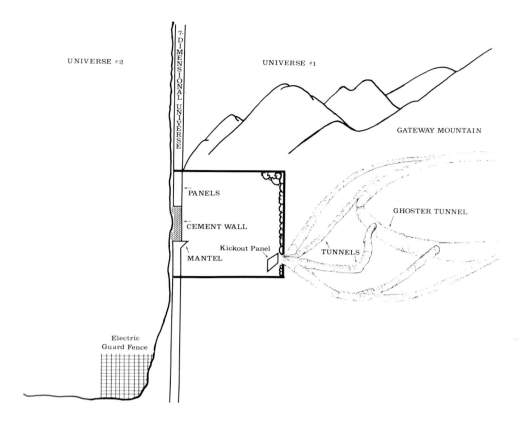

Now, in universe No. 1 (in your world) there are hundreds of feet of rock on the other side of the cement wall: (if people blasted through the wall there'd be no universe No. 2---just solid rock in universe No. 1!).

# UNIVERSE #1

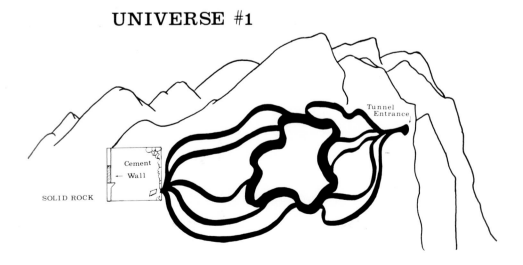

But in the PREVIOUS picture you can see that in universe No. 2 there is merely a straight wall of rock above and below the cement wall, with only air directly on the opposite side of the wall from the one that faces the room. Monsters have a 35' fall to the ground if they come out the wall on that side, so they don't (very often), and even if one did (which they rarely have) live through the fall, they'd NEVER live through the electric charges in the fences. So we're quite safe.

And guess what's on the other side of the cement wall in universe No. 2? (You know, the side that has the room in it in universe No. 1) Solid rock for miles! It's a mountain range. Here's another picture:

# UNIVERSE #2

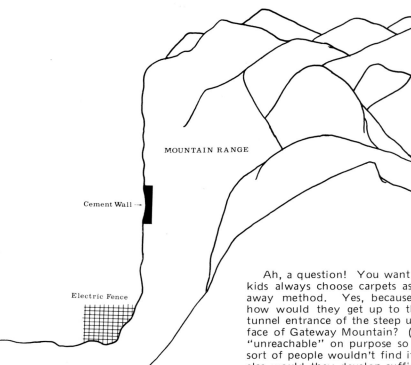

MOUNTAIN RANGE

Cement Wall →

Electric Fence

(How did a panel slide open in Lindsay and Sammy's room? They don't make wall panels that open in kids' rooms. That's a good question---YOU think up the answer! And write it down and send it to the publisher. Best answers will get prizes. They'll be judged for originality, cuteness, logic, and creativity.)

Any more questions? What do you mean you've "fallen asleep"? Didn't you WANT to find out how YOU could get to my world, or at least find out what happens to some of the kids of your world that run away and are never heard from again? Ever hear of U.F.O.'s? SOME of them are simply kids on carpets!

Ah, a question! You want to know if kids always choose carpets as their runaway method. Yes, because otherwise how would they get up to the exterior tunnel entrance of the steep unclimbable face of Gateway Mountain? (We built it "unreachable" on purpose so the wrong sort of people wouldn't find it.) Or how else would they develop sufficient speed (while in the haunted room) to get through the wall? Speed is needed only because the kids' energies are never perfectly 100% high quality, so there IS some RESISTANCE which causes the flash of light.

Which reminds me. The wall was found by my great great great great great great great great great great great great great great great great great great great great great great great great great great great great great great great great great great grandmother Millicent 999 years ago. She was walking near that rock wall with the cement wall 35' high up on it, and saw a monster's face peek out and then go back. She astrally traveled a few blocks into the mountain (by first going through the wall) and instead of arriving in the solid rock of our world's mountain range, as she should have, she was in open air on the far side of a totally unknown mountain (Gateway of universe No. 1, YOUR world).

Over time our people built the room, the tunnel (in which they planted the special nitrogen-consuming moss that glows) and the ghoster---all to give still-turned-on people of your world a chance to find love and peace and happiness.

It's fun to watch the creatures poke their heads out of solid cement and then retreat. Some nights it happens every few seconds. They are so comical!

Now why can't people possessing high-quality energy walk right through the 7-dimensional universe's creatures? They could! Unfortunately, the creatures always end up using 4-dimensional (low quality energy) weapons. Also, during the fear and struggle of the fighting, people's energies are often not of very high quality.

Why not lock the panels at each end of the mantel so the creatures are prevented from entering the haunted room? You've probably already guessed. It's the last and final test before the ultimate test of the total-belief-dropping, total-risking, wall-penetration-attempt. It separates the brave from the cowards.

If one has enough life-wish to care enough to possess high enough quality energy to get through the wall, then one is willing to fight monsters to get to my world. If one knows that running from them means that there's no way to get to my world, but one runs anyway, his/her energy quality level wouldn't have gotten him/her through the wall.

Why don't we influence people telepathically, in your world, so that they start acting with awareness and compassion like they do in my world; and also why not influence them to run around and give each other therapy so that they could "turn back on" and perhaps get to the level of care at which they'd be willing and able to drop all beliefs and get through that wall; and finally, why not influence people in your world with all of my people's psychic powers, in such a way that they cease being so hateful or misunderstanding towards one another? Well, because we believe that people have the right to CHOOSE what happens to them. You don't like your school's saying "do this and that only", without ever giving you a choice in the matter. We don't believe in influencing people, even for the "good", without giving them a choice.

And IF WE ASKED people of your world if they'd like to be "influenced" by us psychics and aliens and ghosts and astral travelers, they'd reach for shotguns as they hollered "NO!" at the top of their lungs!

Let's see now; I promised I'd take a look at the implications of tangency, so let's look at the fact that only at the point of tangency to the cement wall will there be a way to go back and forth between universes No. 1 and No. 2. The cement wall is the ONLY way to get from one to another of our 4-dimensional worlds.

Here's a picture:

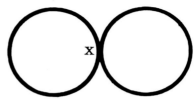

Let the picture represent space-helmets of astronauts. The astronauts have radio failure and no longer can hear each other on their communicators. So what do they do? They touch helmets! The sound vibrations can then get through, which they cannot do in the vacuum of space.

Space's vacuum is a context for the non-existence of sound. Talk all you want, but does COMMUNICATION exist when no one can hear you? No. But it gets through WHEN THEY TOUCH!

Look at the "space-helmet" picture. The point where they touch, x, is called their point of TANGENCY. Now consider that point "x" is as small as a period (.) when 2 circles meet on a page, but as big as a 6-foot-thick and 20'x20' cement wall when 2 universes are "tangent". Of course, if the universes really were tangent they'd be tangent universes, not parallel ones, and at point x ANYONE could go back and forth between universes without any need for intermediary cement walls and 7-dimensional universes. But, luckily, they're not tangent to each other, but merely tangent to the same wall, but on opposite sides.

I wonder if you realize what it would mean to my world if it was tangent to yours? It would mean war, hate, disease, being conquered, etc. At least that's the way I read your history books from universe No. 1. Am I ever GLAD that wall is there!

But let's not dwell on some of the nastier possibilities that a gate between our universes suggests. The fact is: that wall filters out all but people who are willing to risk all and believe nothing in order to get Home, which the still-turned-on children of universe No. 1 desire deeply, profoundly, and to the very depths of their beings.

I have to go now. I've enjoyed sharing all of this with you, and hope that some day you'll know exactly WHY I decided to accept Richard's offer to let you hear about all this.

Love,

Linda

## OTHER BOOKS BY RICHARD M. VIXEN

### Deep Foot

A triumphant, voluptuous novel about a woman's enlightenment. A mercilessly erotic, tenderly passionate journey into love and awareness.

When Lotta escaped from her prison of beliefs (about what she thought her life was *supposed* to be about) she found a whole new world of love and beauty awaiting her, and she fell in love with . . . . . . . . . everyone!

Lotta's awareness grew until she was suddenly confronted with the fact that she *wasn't* stuck with marrying some guy and playing housewife and mother. She could have more----much *MUCH* MORE!! Each book $2.25 plus 45 cents postage & handling.

### Deeper Foot

A literary milestone of shocking beauty. An intense, passionate, sweetly erotic novel of a young woman's soul-searching quest for a way to reach a whole world with her unprecedented love of life and people.

Titania was one of the first people in this world who had been brought up perfectly. Her environment, with all of its loving people and compassionate space for being, offered unprecedented choices, freedom, being-space.

At 18 she went out into the world on her own--- a world full of barriers, defenses, oppression and misery. She was willing to risk all to reach the world with her compassion. Her intense life-passions warmed everyone she met, a warmth that melted barriers and inspired the very souls of her new friends. Each book $2.25 plus 45 cents postage & handling.